Picking

3   D1424751

PAVILION

This book has
been adopted by

....

who will give it a
loving home forever

For Bill and Eddie, with love PF
For Fay and Trevor, with love CV

First published in the United Kingdom in 2018 by
Pavilion Children's Books
43 Great Ormond Street
London WC1N 3HZ

An imprint of Pavilion Books Limited.

Publisher and Editor: Neil Dunnicliffe; Art Director: Anna Lubecka

Illustrations © Clara Vulliamy 2018
Text © Polly Faber 2018

The moral rights of the author and illustrator have been asserted

ISBN: 9781843653554

10 9 8 7 6 5 4 3 2

Reproduction by Mission Productions Ltd, Hong Kong
Printed by IMAK Ofset Ltd, Turkey

This book can be ordered directly from the publisher online at www.pavilionbooks.com, or try your local bookshop.

Picking Pickle

by Polly Faber & Clara Vulliamy

Hello!

Have *you* come to choose a dog?

How exciting!

Picking can be tricky though.
Can I help?
I've been here the longest.
I know *everyone*.

I'll find the perfect
match for you.
Let me sniff...

...mmmm – you smell *lovely*.

Come and meet

Geraldo.

He's *very* handsome.

He's won prizes;

rosettes and a silver cup.

BEST IN
SHOW

He enjoys a stroke
of those silky ears –
go on!

But *are* those his ears or...

the other end?

You wouldn't want to get it wrong.

How about

HARVEY?

We all

look up

to Harvey.

He's got quite an appetite.

Did I smell *treats* in your pocket?

Harvey may have smelled them too.

You might need
to give him one.

Or two...

or three... or

HARVEY!

And here is **Dumpling.**

She's *ever* so clever.

She chews through news,
opinions *and* the crossword
in seconds.

She speaks five different languages!

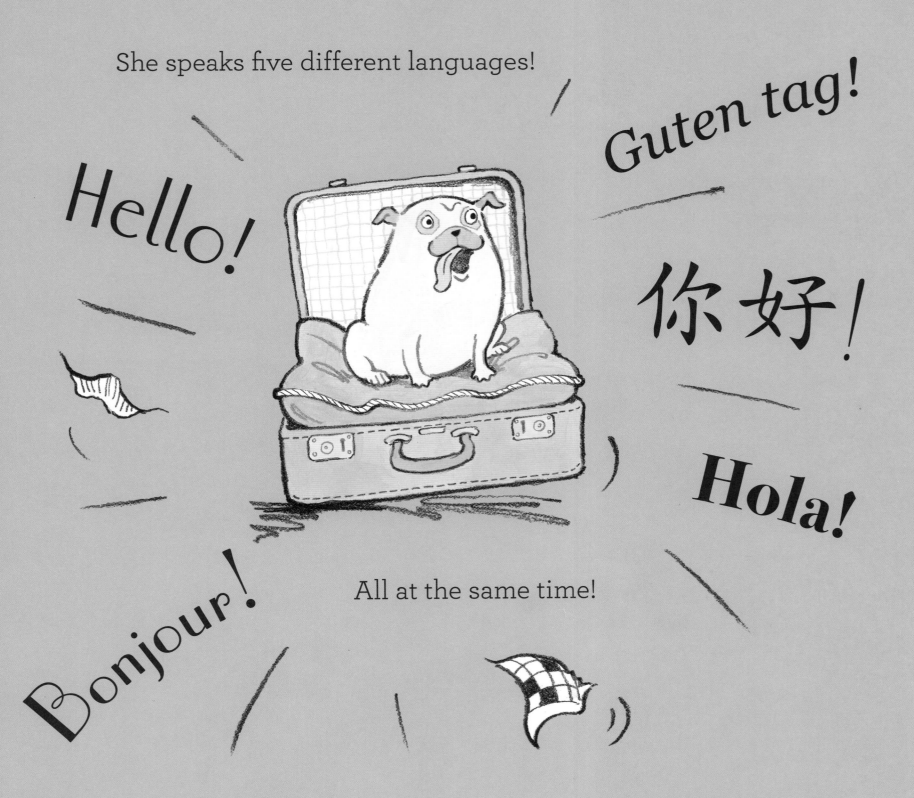

Guten tag!

Hello!

你好!

Hola!

Bonjour!

All at the same time!

But I haven't asked...

...what do you need your dog to do?

If you're after a guard or

a working animal you'll find

Matilda

has *marvellous* teeth.

WIGGINS

is *very* good at...

HOOOOWL!

loudness!

And **Dibble**

can round up *anything!*

You brought a ball? My favourite!

Can I bring it back?

Can I bring it back again?

Can I bring it
back *again?*

For sporty fun you must meet

BOO-BOO!

Boo-Boo almost *is* a ball, he's so bouncy.

Boo-Boo! Come back Boo-Boo!

BOO-BOO?

BOO-BOO!

He is *fast*.

Have a rest.

This is trickier
than usual.

A tummy rub for me?

Why thank you! I *love* them.

Ahhh...

You deserve the best of all.

And the *best* dog here is *definitely*...

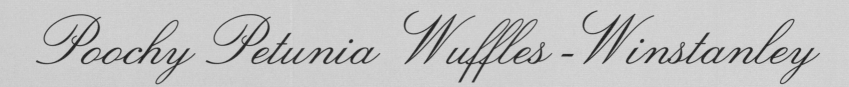

Poochy Petunia Wuffles - Winstanley

Poochy Petunia

100% PURE PEDIGREE

You can see she has breeding.

Look at her nose!

Look at her certificate in a frame!

She is waiting for someone perfect.

Someone like you.

Small questions:

Can you offer a golden bowl?

A diamond collar?

Tea at the Palace every week?

Now *that* isn't good manners.
I'm so sorry.

I don't know what to say.
I can't understand it.

Is there no dog
here that's right?
This *is* a pickle.

What's that?

You *have* chosen? You know *exactly* who you want to take home forever?

Oh.

That's... good news.

Very good news.

I'm happy for them.

Tell me please;

who is it to be?